Written by JD Green
Illustrated by Jennifer Naalchigar
Designed by Nicola Moore

First published by HOMETOWN WORLD in 2018
Hometown World Ltd
7 Northumberland Buildings
Bath
BA1 2JB

www.hometownworld.co.uk

Follow us @hometownworldbooks

ARCHIE YOU'RE AMAZING!

Hometown World

Archie is so **helpful**.

He gives this mix a beating.

SPLAT!

And when that cake's had time to bake,

he'll help out **with**

the

eating.

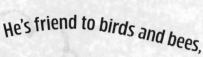

Archie is so **caring**.

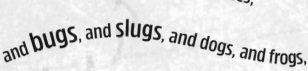

He's friend to birds and bees,

and **bugs**, and **slugs**, and dogs, and frogs,

and even **cats with fleas!**

PING!

Archie is a **rOck Star!**

Each time he hears a song,

he sings aloud but does not care

if all the words are wrong!

Archie has a **lovely** smile

that goes from ear to ear.

Just being around Archie

leaves you feeling full of cheer.

Archie is so **sporting**.
You'll always see him **grinning**.

Not **everything** comes easily.

He practises **a lot!**

And that's how he's developed

the **AMAZING** skills he's got.

Archie is a **brave** boy.

This spider's **not** a threat!

He picks it up, **gives it a name**

and keeps it as **his pet!**

There's always **fun** and **laughter**
wherever Archie goes.

He likes to dance around a lot
and strike a funky pose...

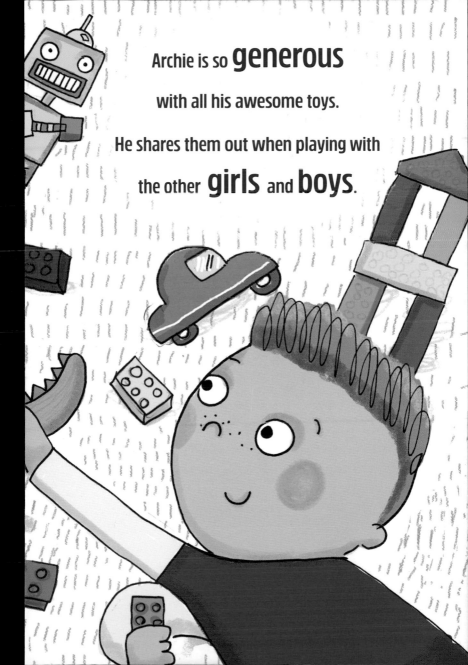

Archie is so **generous** with all his awesome toys.

He shares them out when playing with the other **girls** and **boys**.

THE BEST!

Archie Is **AMAZING**.

What sets this boy apart

is that he's **cool**, and **brave**, and **fun**,

and has a **GREAT**

BIG

HEART!

Add some more
AMAZING
words about
YOU!